To Ramona Margaret Wheeler Korn
M. B.

To my highly creative dad
I. A.

First published 2019 by Walker Books Ltd
87 Vauxhall Walk, London SE11 5HJ

This edition published 2020

2 4 6 8 10 9 7 5 3 1

This book has been typeset in Bauer Grotesk

Printed in China

British Library Cataloguing in Publication Data: a catalogue record for this book is available from the British Library

ISBN 978-1-4063-9306-4

www.walker.co.uk

JUST BECAUSE

Mac Barnett

illustrated by

Isabelle Arsenault

WALKER BOOKS

AND SUBSIDIARIES

LONDON • BOSTON • SYDNEY • AUCKLAND

Why is the ocean blue?

Every night,
when you
go to sleep,

the fish
take out
guitars.

They sing sad songs and cry blue tears.

What is
the rain?

The tears
of flying fish.

Why do the leaves change colour?

By winter,
their branches have
all burned up.

Why do birds fly south for the winter?

To fetch

new leaves

for trees.

What happened to the dinosaurs?

Millions of years ago, thousands of asteroids fell on the earth.

But the dinosaurs
had planned for this.
They fastened themselves
to big balloons,
floated up to space,
and stayed there.

What are black holes?

What is
a volcano?

How do
you tame
a horse?

Wha
a dese

What
is the
wind?

How big
was a woolly
mammoth?

What are
freckles?

How were
the pyramids
built?

What is
an echo?

What is
quicksand?

What is
the moon?

What is
a rainbow?

Why do
we sneeze?

How tall
is the tallest
mountain?

How does
an egg become
a chicken?

What is
thunder?

What is
lightning?

Why do we have to sleep?

Because there are some things we can only see with our eyes closed.

Mac Barnett is the author of many books for children. He has collaborated with illustrator Jon Klassen on six titles, which include *Sam and Dave Dig a Hole*, *The Wolf, the Duck and the Mouse*, the Shape trilogy (*Triangle*, *Square* and *Circle*) and *Extra Yarn*, which won a Caldecott Honor and a Boston-Globe Horn Book Award. Mac lives in California, USA.

Isabelle Arsenault has achieved international recognition for her work and won many awards, including the Governor General's Literary Award (three times!). She is the creator of *Alpha* and the illustrator of *Jane, the Fox & Me* by Fanny Britt, a *New York Times* Book Review Best Illustrated Children's Book or the Year, as well as *Captain Rosalie* by Timothée de Fombelle. Isabelle lives in Montreal, Canada.